I dedicate this book to my mother,
who's believed in this story since she first read
it...twenty-years ago.

—EL

I dedicate this book to my
Goddaughter, Freya Leonie Laing.

—JFA

The Squickerwonkers

ISBN: 978-0-9895891-2-3

Published by:

Quiet Cocoon Productions (QCP)

#815 – 16633 Ventura Blvd

Encino, CA

91436

www.thesquickerwonkers.com

Author photo by Sarah Dunn, courtesy of Warner Bros. Pictures

First QCP edition: July 2013

First Titan edition: November 2014

Printed in Heshan

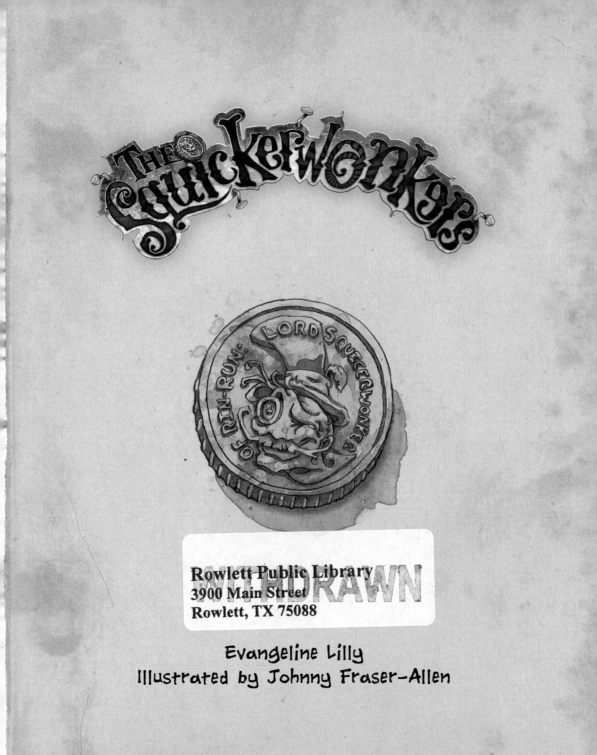

The Squickerwonkers

LORD SQUICKERWONKER OF RUN-RUN

Evangeline Lilly
Illustrated by Johnny Fraser-Allen

There once was a clever and passionate girl
Who wandered away from a fair.
She ventured inside
A wagon-like ride,
And what did she find in there?

"Welcome my dear," said a voice from the wings,
"To the fabulous Squickershow!
You dropped in your coin,
So now you can join.
Come up here and see how it goes."

The girl looked around to see who it was
That spoke with a sinister tone.
But she saw not a soul,
Save a rat in a hole.
It seemed that the girl was alone.

At once there came a noise from above!
Nine figures swung down from the shadows!
Their bodies hung loose
As if strung from a noose,
As if all nine were hanging from gallows!

"Come onto the stage, don't be afraid,
Meet my motley crew.
They may have their vices,
But those are life's spices,
And I suspect...so do you."

"The head of the Squickerwonker troop
Is known as Papa the Proud.
He has terrible airs,
Never mingles or shares
With commoners out in the crowd."

"The colossal woman on his arm,
The crowd calls Mama the Mean.
Just follow the trail,
Of what is derailed,
And that is where Mama has been."

"Then there is Gilligan the Guilty
Who frets and worries all day,
Following his wife,
The love of his life,
Who takes but never does pay."

"Her name is Greer the Greedy
A thief with a great sense of flair,
She loves to pick pockets,
Small purses and lockets
And hide what she finds in her hair."

"And how about Andy the Arrogant?
The hunk of our traveling pack.
He's broad and lean,
A physical dream...
But brains he clearly does lack."

"Let's not forget Lorna the Lazy,
Who mopes all about with a frown.
She hasn't a hobby,
Her knees are all knobby.
She's slovenly, sulky and down."

"Gillis the Gluttonous has a heart of gold,
But a body of doughnuts and pie.
He does all his eating
As if he's competing,
And sadly he's painfully shy."

"Beside him is Sparky the Spectacle,
The ham of our curious brood.
He likes to tell jokes,
Loves ladies and smokes,
And to our dismay, he's quite crude."

"Meghan the Mute is the youngest,
Yet a leader who's hungry for power.
She is wise and sure,
Her intentions are pure,
But her enemies, she will devour!"

"So what do you say," the voice carried on,
"Will you leave or will you engage?"
Though the girl was suspicious,
Her fear felt delicious,
And so she hopped onto the stage!

Wringing their hands, the Squickers crept near
Surrounding the brave little girl,
Then humming a tune,
They popped her balloon
And stepped back to watch her unfurl.

Her eyes, they began to well with hot tears
As she stared at her limp balloon string,
But then the girl's pout
Opened into a shout,
She yelled...

"HOW COULD YOU DO SUCH A THING?!"

"I'm Selma!" she boiled, "of the Rin-Run Royals,
Heir of all that is under the sun.
And I swear you will pay,
For your childish display,
For having your wee bit of fun!"

"When my Gramp hears, you made me shed tears,
He'll punish you all well and true!
And I have no doubt
That he will find out,
For I plan on telling on you!"

She screamed and she yelled, with fists in the air,
And threw an incredible fit.
She bellowed and moaned,
She kicked and she groaned,
And just when they thought she might quit...

From up in the rafters, a new puppet dropped
Who looked just like Selma's old gramp!
Dark magic was stirring
Strange things were occurring
By the light of the kerosene lamps!

With buttons for eyes and with straw for his hair
Puppet Gramp appeared by Selma's side,
And in the girl's fury,
Her vision was blurry,
So she turned to that puppet and cried:

"They popped my beautiful red balloon,
And for this you must have their heads!"
The Squickers drew near
And with voices sincere,
Begged her, "Won't you show mercy instead?"

Gramp had a think,
then shot Selma a wink
And said, "Here's what I'll
do with this lot."
She looked them all over,
From block foot to shoulder,
"Oh goody,
these Squickers are caught."

...Selma thought.

"Although I love my Selma dear,"
Puppet Gramp began to explain,
"She's spoiled to her core,
And a constant chore,
So I'll speak in terms very plain..."

"If you take this girl into your
group,
And love her as if she's your own,
If you give her your care,
I'll make you the heirs
Of the Rin-Run family throne."

With those choice words,
a change did take place
Taking Selma the Spoiled by surprise.
Her strings were attached,
Her clothes became patched
And she suddenly
had coins for eyes!

The shock on her face turned quickly to rage
As she mustered a miserable scream.
Without hesitation,
With determination,
They muzzled that scream as a team.

"She'll be perfectly fine, just leave her to us."

"We know how to love a spoiled child."

"You can utterly trust, It won't be a bust."

"We're mad for a child that is wild."

Happy with that, Puppet Gramp slipped away,
Leaving Selma to think he'd gone bonkers!
But her fate had been sealed,
Her dark nature revealed,
She was one of the strange Squickerwonkers!

JOHNNY FRASER★ALLEN is a senior sculptor and conceptual designer at WETA Workshop where he has worked since his teens. His film credits include Andrew Adamson's Narnia Chronicles, Stephen Spielberg's Tintin, and Peter Jackson's King Kong and The Hobbit Trilogy.

Johnny is currently working on a series of illustrated Young Adult novels titled The Gloaming Trilogy: www.thegloamingtrilogy.com You can follow The Gloaming Trilogy on facebook for book release updates and current exhibition dates.

Special Thanks to: Jim Henson who taught me of Dragons, for my mum and pop who carried me to their eyries, and for Richard Taylor who taught me how to fly them, thank you.

Special mention to Tania Rodger and Guillermo Del Toro for believing in me and nurturing my work, and a big thank you to Max Patté, Rob Baldwin, Amy Fitzgerald, Joy Buckle, Mary Pike, Tristan McCallum, Emma Bartlett, Katherine Tuttle, Tiger Von Stormborn and especially Nick and Claire Laing, could not have got this far without any of you.

I dedicate this book to my Goddaughter, Freya Leonie Laing.

"And so the girl learned, on that fateful night,
Not to be too quick to judge,
There's a devil inside, you might like to hide,
...But what if I gave it a nudge?"